First published 2015 by Walker Books Ltd ◆ 87 Vauxhall Walk, London SE11 5HJ ◆ 2 4 6 8 10 9 7 5 3

Text © 2015 Jonathan Emmett ◆ Illustrations © 2015 Vanessa Cabban ◆ The right of Jonathan Emmett and Vanessa Cabban to be identified
as author and illustrator respectively of this work has been asserted by them in accordance with the Copyright, Designs and Patents Act 1988
You can find out more about Jonathan Emmett's books by visiting his website at www.scribblestreet.co.uk ◆ This book has been typeset in
Contemporary Brush ◆ Printed in China ◆ All rights reserved. No part of this book may be reproduced, transmitted or stored in an information
retrieval system in any form or by any means, graphic, electronic or mechanical, including photocopying, taping and recording,
without prior written permission from the publisher. ◆ British Library Cataloguing in Publication Data: a catalogue record for this book
is available from the British Library ◆ ISBN 978-1-4063-4799-9 ◆ www.walker.co.uk

WALKER BOOKS
AND SUBSIDIARIES

LONDON ◆ BOSTON ◆ SYDNEY ◆ AUCKLAND

A Spot of Bother

Jonathan Emmett

Vanessa Cabban

It was a fine summer morning on Hilltop Farm
and Pig was enjoying a breakfast of big, juicy cherries.

"Yum, yum!" said Pig
as he finished his meal.

Pig was very proud of his appearance
and always kept himself perfectly clean.
So he was horrified to see that a squashed cherry
had left a bright red spot on his side.

It was only a small spot,
but once Pig had noticed it
he couldn't ignore it. And, try as he might,
he could not get at it to clean it off.

"Good morning, Pig!" said Goat,
who wandered by chewing something.

"It's not a 'good morning'!" said Pig.
"Can't you see this bothersome spot?"

"It's a MONSTROUS MISFORTUNE!" said Pig.

"Don't worry," said Goat, "I'll soon clean it off!"

And he began licking at the spot.

Goat finished
licking ...

and stepped back
to take a look.

"Sorry, Pig!"
said Goat guiltily.

"It must have been
the beetroot I was eating."

"It's a TERRIBLE TRAGEDY!" moaned Pig.

"Don't worry," said Cow, "I'll soon clean it off!"

Cow fetched a mop from the tractor shed.

And she rubbed it on the spot.

Cow finished
rubbing ...

and stepped back
to take a look.

"Sorry, Pig!"
said Cow contritely.

"There must have been some
tractor oil on that mop."

"It's a DREADFUL DISASTER!"
wailed Pig.

"Don't worry," said Sheep,
"I'll soon clean it off!"

Sheep led Pig
to the sheep dip.

And poured shampoo
on the spot.

Sheep finished
shampooing ...

and Pig climbed
out to take a look.

"Sorry, Pig!"
said Sheep sheepishly.

"That shampoo — it must have
been sheep dye."

"It's a CALAMITOUS CATASTROPHE!"
howled Pig.

"At least now you're all one colour,"
said Cow.

"I think blue rather suits you,"
said Goat.

"So do I," agreed Sheep.

"No, it doesn't! I look like
a giant blueberry!"
blurted Pig.

Pig couldn't bear for anyone
to look at him, so he ran off
and hid in the barn.

He didn't come out until it was dark and, even then, he crept around the edge of the farm so that no one would see him.

Unfortunately, it was SO dark that Pig couldn't see where he was going and before he knew it, he'd fallen into a big, muddy puddle.

By the time he'd crawled
out again, he was covered
from head to trotter
in thick, sticky mud.

"Just when I thought it couldn't
get any worse," groaned Pig,
as he trudged back to his shelter
and collapsed in a dejected heap.

When Cow, Goat and Sheep got up the next day,

Pig was nowhere to be seen.

They spent the whole morning looking for him,

but the only clue they found was a big heap of mud

next to his shelter.

They were inspecting this curiously

when it spoke to them.

"Go away!"
said the heap
grumpily.

The other animals gasped in surprise as Pig raised his muddy head.

"I didn't think things could get any worse than they were yesterday, but look at me now!" grumbled Pig.

The hot sun had dried out the mud
so that it cracked and fell off as Pig
got to his feet and shuffled away.

"But Pig!" said Cow.

"You look FANTASTIC!" said Goat.

"I don't think I've ever seen you looking so clean!" agreed Sheep.

And it was true, the mud had sucked out all the dye and dirt from the day before, leaving Pig ...

COMPLETELY CLEAN!

Pig could not believe it at first, but when he realized
it was true, he danced with delight. "I'm spotless!
I'm speckless! I'm pinker than pink!

I'm a PERFECTLY PRISTINE PIG!"
he shouted as he pranced
to and fro in front
of his friends.

He'd just finished with a flourish
when he felt something sticking to his bottom.
"What is it?" he said, straining to look.

"It looks like a squashed cherry,"
said Cow.

Goat swallowed the mouthful
of beetroot he'd been chewing
and licked his lips.
"Don't worry," he said,
"I'll soon clean it off..."

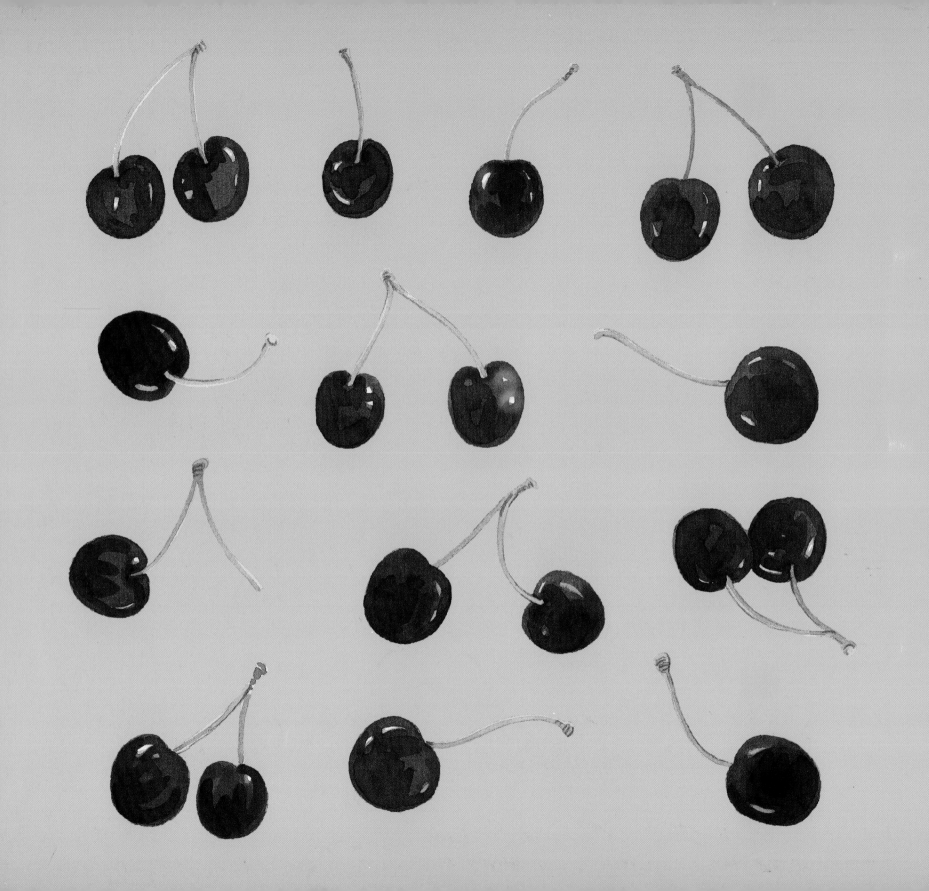